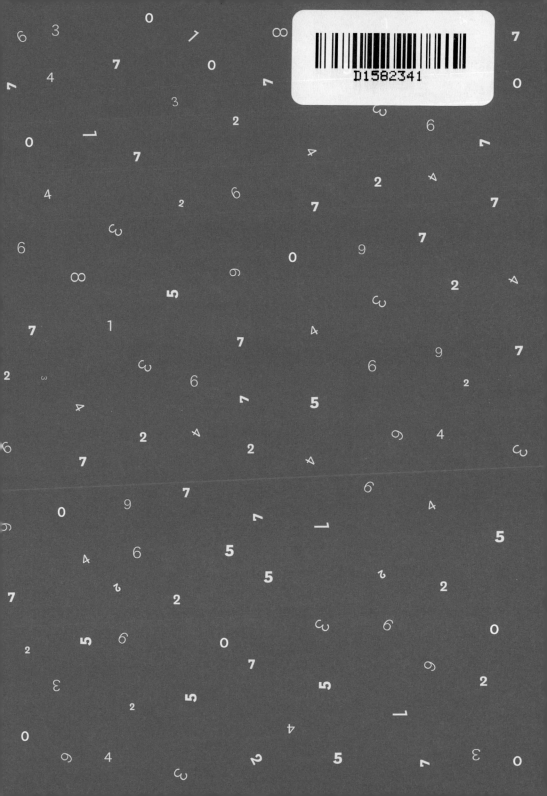

MIKE MASILAMANI

Th3 8oy
Who 5p3ak5
1n Numb3r5

Art: Matthew Frame

t

All Internally Displaced Persons (IDPs) were detained in closed camps. Massive overcrowding led to terrible conditions, breaching the basic social and economic rights of the detainees, and many lives were lost unnecessarily.

—

Report of the United Nation Secretary General's panel of experts on accountability in Sri Lanka, Executive Summary, April 2011

To Kethaki and Mandeep

Numbers speak very softly — but they always have something important to share. It is best not to ignore the numbers when they speak.

1

If at any point in the following story you are to feel dizzy, out of breath, light-headed, disoriented, and of the growing suspicion that you are lost, it's probably true. It's easy to lose your way in the Island of Short Memories between questionable plans and careful scheming. To mistake those in the army of the Winning Team for the actual villains. Or to confuse the Little Tin Soldiers who are constantly looking out for youth of fighting age, with the inmates of the Kettle Camp who got old overnight.

The Kettle Camp looks like a tin-pot kingdom run by a tin-pot dictator; corrugated tin sheets make the endless rows of tin sheds, tin pots serve the food, tin buckets distribute water, which comes in a big tinny bowser — if lucky, once a day — over the flimsy tin bridge that sticks out like a spout into nowhere.

There is tin everywhere. Too much tin and too much sun make the camp unbearably hot during the day. In the evenings the tin sheets will hiss and crackle and at night the wind blows through them, with a peculiar whistle.

It reminds him of a giant patched-up kettle. The Boy Who Speaks in Numbers has never seen anything like it.

In the far corner of the camp there is a tiny field, in which the inmates exercise and The Boy will soon play Silly Cricket — except when it rains. It has one ugly tree that doesn't give any shade. At each corner there are guard posts with searchlights. The inmates joke that it is always daylight at the Kettle Camp.

Now as the hero of this story, you would expect the Boy Who Speaks in Numbers to be an imposing figure, but the truth is he is small and insignificant, striking not a heroic pose, but looking very sorry for himself — his finger stuck deep up his nose. The Boy is thinking.

Whenever he is deep in thought, he has his finger stuck up his nose.

The Boy has arrived there along with the Kind Uncle after many days' journey, sidestepping landmines and snakes. Their treacherous journey to the Kettle Camp has taken weeks in the company of this weary line of broken people; their stride broken, their pride seeping out, their words coming out in strangled sobs.

There are too many of them to count; too many still not comprehending that for the rest of their lives, they will never know another home.

They are bent, not by the burden of possessions, but by the weight of recent memory. They are Innocent Deceived People (IDPs) and they aren't pretty to look at. They are all headed to the Kettle Camp.

But they aren't the reason he is sad. He isn't thinking of the IDPs at all. He is missing the Constantly Complaining Cow and his home at the Small Village of Fat Hopes.

But we are getting ahead of our story, and the journey of the Boy who flees his village to escape the Civil War of Lies. The same village that the national TV channel CMYK would one day describe as being at 'at the far north of our island and the wrong end of the barrel'.

2

Look as you may, you won't find it on a map. Because of the Civil War of Lies, the Small Village of Fat Hopes — somewhere near the False Dividing Line (FDL) — has grown famous for all the wrong reasons. They speak in colour in the village, as they do in most parts of the Island of Short Memories. The cost of living makes people purple, people are often marooned, and the jokes are all black.

The Boy Who Speaks in Numbers on the other hand, knows only numbers. He knows them well. He knows that numbers are not yellow and loud. They don't speed around. They don't overpower you with their perfume (like pinks tend to do). He knows numbers to be polite and well mannered. They are his best friends at the village.

As easily as other children are able to name their favourite cars, the Boy and the children of the Small Village are able to name the war planes that fly low overhead — and the big guns that are fired at them. But the children of the Small Village still can't tell the good people from the bad people.

That was not all they can't tell. They can't tell:
1) Why no one visits their village anymore.
2) Where the other children have gone.
3) Why they feel like outsiders in their own village.
4) Where all these checkpoints have come from.

The Boy is taking a walk, making sure he avoids the Singing Fridges Checkpoint. Uninviting as it looks, the Singing Fridges Checkpoint is said to belong to a fast expanding chain, the Checkpoint Corporation, one of those new companies that has come up with the war. In its time the Singing Fridges Checkpoint had been feared and spoken of far and wide, but business is dull now — no one wants to come to the Small Village of Fat Hopes anymore.

Ordinary as they look with tin sheets and sandbags, checkpoints are good business. Their main source of income is the bribes made to come into the village and the bribes made to leave. The more creative have other sources of taxing the villagers — from a cow that moos too loud to cycles exceeding the speed limit.

A checkpoint at the right junction can make as much business, if not more, than a tea shop. Unlike tea shops though, the trick is to look as threatening as possible, which with the right sponsor, is not all that difficult. (Which also explains why later in life, the Boy could never open a Singing Fridge without an involuntary shudder.)

The checkpoints serve as constant reminders that they are strangers in their own village.

It is a quiet day. No birds chirp, no guns boom. The Boy puts as much distance as he can between himself and Singing Fridges. He is heading in the general direction of the Yes Yes Store (whatever you ask, the answer is always 'Yes, Yes'), when he hears something odd.

It sounds like an animal in distress but at the same time like '60 rupees a kilo of red rice!'

The grumblings get louder:

'300 rupees a kilo of flour!'

Then, 'Canned fish 500 rupees!'

Or is it a muffled moo?

He isn't sure but it seems to come from round the next corner. The Boy rushes round to discover a cow hopping about in a very un-cow-like fashion with her hind legs stuck in a roll of barbed wire.

'980 rupees a kilo of dried fish! Moo! 500 rupees a packet of milk!' complains the Constantly Complaining Cow, as the Boy gently releases her and strokes her head. Her big eyes shining with gratitude, she nuzzles him and continues 'Soap 25 rupees, 180 rupees a litre of coconut oil, Moo! 640 rupees a kilo of tea! Amoo!'

The Boy wants to hear more and invites her to join him for tea at the Southern Tea Shop ('Famous also in the East and the West').

They make an odd pair, but soon are a regular feature there. The Boy sips plain tea and the Complaining Cow chomps on a banana, while she regales him with stories such as '80 rupees a kilo of Bombay onions, chillies at 500 rupees!' and other such incredible tales.

3

'Help! I'm caught in a minefield!'

In his usual trusting manner, the Boy Who Speaks in Numbers is about to investigate the call, but the Complaining Cow stops him with a roll of her eyes. Sure enough, they soon come across the Lying Lizard, sunning himself on a rock. He isn't really a lizard; he just looks like one, only bigger (Maximus Lapsus Linguae). He says he is from the Ministry of Internal Revisions, recently posted to the Small Village of Fat Hopes.

To impress the ladies he will sing:

Once I was much celebrated
Now I'm newly liberated.
Oh jubilation!
War has its own
Compensation!
I am a lizard
Newly liberated!

He is neither tuneful nor convincing.

The Lizard also has bad breath, but the Boy doesn't mind. After all, numbers smell too, though mostly of chalk and stale classrooms but sometimes they smell of over-ripe mangoes.

Someone once told the Lizard that lots of sunlight could cure his bad breath, but there is no cure for his lying. Even he knows that. Every time the Lizard speaks, he lies; he can't help himself as much as he can't help his bad breath.

In addition to being a skilled liar, he can change colour dramatically when needed. Currently, he is a dirty shade of grey, with muddy brown splotches. He has a filthy hangover to match.

"Hey, did you hear about the Humanitarian Mission?" he asks the Boy and the Complaining Cow.

"Dried fish 980 Rupees! Amoo! Another mission but why?"

"Why, to liberate civilians!" A blue vein pulses in the Lizard's forehead.

"Sugar 300 rupees! From what?"

"From the grip of war!" he says, red stars rising in his tail.

"Bombay onions 90 rupees! But how can war...?" begins the Cow, and gives up.

"It's true the number of casualties looks alarming right now," cuts in the Lizard, moving into the shade, and leaving a trail of bad breath. "But my department is working on it!"

"Chilli powder 100 rupees! Your department?"

"Yes, the Department of Census and Consensus. We are making great progress recruiting Zero Heroes!" says the Lizard importantly, with green circles under his eyes.

"But how..." starts the Boy.

"If everyone agrees to have the numbers reduced to a zero, then we will truly be a nation of Zero Heroes," interrupts the Lizard, now in the shade, back to his earlier dirty shade of grey. "That day will be marked as Zero Heroes' Day!" he concludes.

For some reason, a riddle his Kind Uncle had once asked him — "What is it that counts for something, yet really stands for nothing?" — comes to his mind. The Boy ducks a wave of bad breath and chucks a stone at the big rock in disgust. There is a loud explosion, and the Lizard leaps up in the air. He *had* been in a minefield, and hadn't been lying for once.

4

The Boy Who Speaks in Numbers is thinking; you could tell by how he has his finger stuck up his nose. It is a habit that the Boy shares with the Kind Uncle. Numbers come easily to them, especially when each has his finger stuck deep up his nose.

The more time the Boy spends with numbers, the more impressed he is by how polite and co-operative they are. Numbers don't know to shade the truth, as people do with colours. As a result, numbers are not always popular, but that doesn't bother them — numbers just go on being numbers. They always have a lesson to offer, however hard the sum, as the Kind Uncle points out.

Uncle and the Boy can often be seen exploring numbers by the stream, at the roadside, in the school grounds; Uncle using piles of mangoes or drawing with a stick to make a point. The Kind Uncle teaches the Boy all he knows about numbers.

Like all villages caught up in the Civil War of Lies, the Small Village has lost most of its youth, including many women. The remaining women are wiser for their sufferings and stronger for their losses, and even as everything collapses around them, they are the glue that keeps the village together. They work hard to put food on the plate, keep everyone's spirits up and their own fears well-disguised.

Their main source of relief is the Hot Gossip Well, where they exchange village scandal with hoots of laughter and much exaggeration. Whatever else they have lost, they have not lost the ability to fabricate stories and create mischief — through recipes, gardening tips, medical advice, shopping bargains, school updates and grooming hints.

5

One day the Boy Who Speaks in Numbers and the Kind Uncle are returning from a walk, fingers still deep into their noses. Around them, the Small Village of Fat Hopes is settling in for the evening. The farmers are putting away their cattle, the traders are counting their money and the women airing their dirty linen at the Hot Gossip Well.

Suddenly they hear a low, long whistle followed by a catcall of big shells. They start running, but the shells begin to land before they get far, the fear still caught in their throats. The Boy is running towards home but the Kind Uncle stops him and pushes him in the opposite direction.

The air smells of gunpowder, the sky quickly filling with evil-eyed clouds of black smoke. Then come the bombers. The first time around, their load breaks in mid-air, spilling a grey storm of harm into the hurting sky. The next time, they dig holes in the ground, flinging dirt and misery the size of houses high into the air. In case anything or anyone still dare move, the bombs come a third time — white-knuckled and phosphorous — and pound them into the ground.

As they keep running, suddenly orphaned toddlers stand in the path of the Kind Uncle and the Boy, bawling for attention above the noise. The flames make weird pictures and fry their imagination, burning everything around them, till they get to the empty Jolly Ice Cream Checkpoint ('Fully Jolly, available in three fevers').

The Boy and his Kind Uncle watch helplessly as the shells keep pounding the village until the next morning. The Civil War of Lies has come in full force to the Small Village of Fat Hopes.

'?? w7y?,w7y?? w7y?? ' cries the Boy.

But that day the numbers are silent; as if the truth is so awful, even the numbers refuse to add them up.

The Kind Uncle too is silent, but for different reasons. Reasons that we can only guess at and will remain forever unknown. The day the night spills red over the Small Village of Fat Hopes is the day the Kind Uncle becomes the Kind Uncle Who Never Speaks. Ever.

6

The Boy Who Speaks in Numbers can't understand where his family has gone. The Small Village of Fat Hopes has turned into a big house of mourning. For once, the Boy can't find comfort in numbers.

The idle chatter of the village has been replaced by loud wailing, and the aimless passage of villagers has been replaced by listless rows of bodies. Bodies crudely tagged with no consideration for family or position. The few identifiable faces seem to have embraced death reluctantly, howling for those left behind. They all look defeated.

The school has turned into a hospital, its passages crowded with the injured. The market place is now a mortuary, fresh murder on display. The survivors have a guarded expression, as if they fear their faces would show too much of the horror they have seen. They clutch their loved ones tightly to themselves, keeping their eyes down and speaking in hoarse whispers. The Constantly Complaining Cow is missing.

The Boy passes the village temple, now a burnt offering. He keeps walking, away from the Happy Hilten Checkpoint ('Friderice and Rose Chicken', it reads), till he comes to the jungle outside the village and discovers that the night has got there ahead of him. He turns back in confusion; all the familiar landmarks are gone. The Gossip Well, the Yes Yes Store, the Southern Tea Shop — 'famous also in the East and West', nothing remains.

The Boy feels very alone. He is lost in his own hometown and can't find the numbers to describe what he is feeling.

Where is the Constantly Complaining Cow when he needs someone to complain to?

He notices the warning signs for the first time, pointing out the poisonous crop of landmines around the village. He decides his best bet is to stay where he is. The jungle comes alive with strange night sounds. The Boy wants to cry. Then he hears a different sound; one that doesn't belong to the jungle. The sound gets closer, sounding like grumblings from the undergrowth. He tries to stop his heart from beating so loudly... when he hears a familiar complaint: '1200 rupees a bag of cement!'

"Th2nkyou, th2nkyou!" He says gratefully to the Constantly Complaining Cow, who leads him back to the Small Village of Fat Hopes, only to find the village deserted except for the Kind Uncle.

From the look in his uncle's eyes, he knows the time has come for them to leave too.

7

The Boy Who Speaks in Numbers is finally to come face to face with the Important Aunty. This Aunty rules the Kettle Camp, where the Boy and his Kind Uncle — turned the Kind Uncle Who Never Speaks — have arrived, carried along by the stream of refugees.

The Cow has refused to make the journey, claiming she is too old to travel. Not all the Boy's tearful protests will make her change her mind. She wishes him well though, joking that he is likely to meet more rounded numbers, the more he travels.

Aunty makes sure the people in the camp never forget how unlucky they are and she never misses a chance to remind them how unfair she is. They are dependent on her for their unhappiness.

But before he meets the Aunty, he has to meet the Important Peons. The Peons play a big role at the Kettle Camp; some say, as important a role as Aunty herself.

It is difficult to tell one Peon from another, but the Boy soon discovers that each has his own personality. There is the Impish, the Imperious and the Impulsive. There is also the Impatient, the Impractical, the Importunate and last but equally lamentable, the Impotent Important Peon. Notwithstanding their individual personalities, their response to any requests invariably is 'Impossible!'

The Boy has been warned by the Peons that Aunty doesn't like questions. Questions give her pimples. She hates pimples; when she gets pimples, she will start scolding in rhyme with no reason. There is nothing more upsetting than when she scolds in rhyme with no reason, the Peons warn the Boy.

Aunty's office is the same size as the other tin sheds and just as hot, marked only by a sign that hangs at the door:

'!ssergorPnigniteeMtnatropml'

She is reading an Important File seated in a chair that once was important but now has an arm missing, at the end of an important table that goes on forever.

The phone rings importantly. The Peons look disapprovingly at him as they scurry in and out with more important files, which they pile on the table, adding to its importance. He is sweating and it isn't only due to the heat. The important files rise to the tin roof like loaves of bread. They smell stale.

"Name?" the Important Aunty finally asks.

"boY," he says weakly.

Aunty takes her face out of the Important File and brings it within inches of his face. He finds himself gazing at a perfectly round face that looks as if it is floating over the rest of her, like a runaway full moon. It is a perfectly smooth face, not a blemish or pimple. She screws up her perfectly round nose.

"I don't want your number, I want your name!" Aunty says through clenched teeth.

"Num3rm2any!" he offers in desperation.

An important meeting is called. The Peons cease their running in and out, and meet around the important table to discuss the fate of the Boy Who Speaks in Numbers.

But before that, the sign 'Important Meeting in Progress!' is turned the right way. The Boy is completely ignored.

One Peon suggests it is impolite of the boy not to speak in colour like the rest of them. Another says he is being impertinent. The others are quick to agree and in one voice chorus their feelings about the Boy staying in the Camp.

"Impossible!" is what they say.

The matter should have ended there and along with that the Boy's stay at the Kettle, until he innocently asks "W6y?"

The question is out of the Boy's mouth before he realises it. Aunty sits back in her once important chair and narrows her little button eyes. There is a sudden hush.

Then with a sick 'plop!' a pimple forces its way through, right on the top of her perfectly round nose. Her little button eyes instantly cross as she tries to look down the end of her nose. The Boy shrinks in his seat even as the Peons inhale sharply.

Then 'plop!' comes another pimple. And soon another. Making her no longer perfectly round nose glow like a lantern. The Important Aunty puffs her perfectly round cheeks. Her crossed little button eyes disappear. Her perfectly round and now impossibly big cheeks begin to quiver. Then she explodes:

Ding dong the mouse
ran down came
a blackbird
killed all the mice,
so the poor little doggie
had hickory dickory dock!

She snarls as she bangs the Important File close, spilling important papers everywhere.

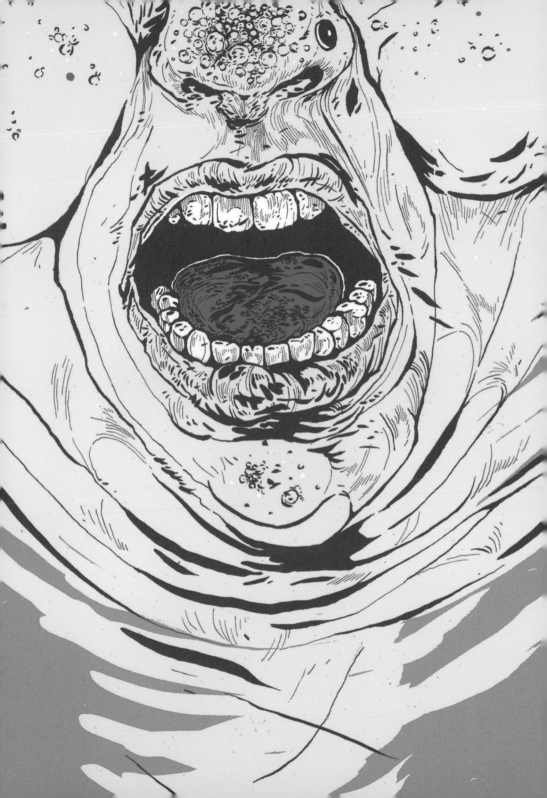

The Peons know the signs well and cover their ears. It is what they fear most — the Aunty scolding in rhyme with no reason.

The Peons — even Importunate and Impotent — flee the office with the Boy in tow. The important meeting comes to a hurried end, the interview with the Boy temporarily adjourned, but Aunty hasn't finished scolding:

I met a crooked man
who wouldn't say his prayers,
had a wife and couldn't keep her,
the cupboard was bare
I took him by the left leg
and threw him down the stairs!

8

Then come the monsoon rains, a muddy downpour that leaves everything wet and everyone grumpy, forcing them all indoors into their already cramped quarters. Even the snakes seek shelter with them with poisonous results. The Kettle is cut off from the rest of the Island of Short Memories and no food or medicines can come through. With the rains come the buzzing mosquitoes, bringing sickness with them.

The inmates of the Kettle go into a sullen silence, not clear whom to trust, not sure whom to blame, only knowing that they are a long way from home.

Thanks to the rains, the Boy is temporarily forgotten. Aunty has other things on her mind — starting with how to stop the Kettle from overflowing.

But just as suddenly, the rains stop. The sun is shining when the inmates wake up one morning to a strange sight. The ugly tree in the playing ground is flowering. It is flowering with questions.

'Is war a wholesale business?' it asks.

The people in the camp start talking again, repeating the question but getting no answers.

On another day it asks, 'Does war make an orphan of hope?' to which the orphans in the camp have a lot to say.

'Is truth a refugee?' it asks on yet another day, which has the Kettle all heated up.

They call the tree the Question Tree.

Aunty objects to the questions — and the pimples that come with it — scolding:

Ding dong the clock
Struck one
Two buckle my shoe!

The Peons — even Importunate and Impotent — go around beating possible suspects, but that doesn't stop the Question Tree from continuing to bloom with refreshing but awkward questions that have a bittersweet fragrance to them.

'Whose war is this anyway?' it asks the day the culprit is produced.

To the dismay of the Boy, it turns out to be the Kind Uncle Who Never Speaks. Before the Boy could protest, Aunty reads out the confession he has signed, her pimples glowing like a lantern. Too late he remembers something his Kind Uncle had told him long ago — "However awkward the questions, it is important to ask them."

The shelling keeps following them, (with one lie leading to another, the Civil War of Lies has got worse), and the Question Tree begins to die. A week later, the Kind Uncle Who Never Speaks disappears. The people of the Kettle go back to their former silence, now heavy with sadness.

With truly large numbers, many odd coincidences are likely to happen, the Kind Uncle has taught the Boy. He has said it was the law of large numbers. When all the people in the Kettle Camp all lost hope at the same time, is that also a coincidence, wonders the Boy.

The Question Tree has one last question:

'War is dumb — is that why we keep silent?'

But no one has any answers.

9

There are different kinds of suffering at the Kettle Camp. There are those who have lost their limbs and there are those who have lost all hope. This includes the Cook who cries in Silence, the Priest without a Prayer, the Barber with a Bad Mood, the Mirror Lady who goes around collecting seven years of bad luck, the Mad Uncle with a Mynah and many Mothers missing a Child.

The hope has been beaten out of them, leaving them hollow-cheeked and hungry. Their future is closing in on them like the tin sheets that make their new home. They have nothing to look forward to.

There is of course no shortage of people looking for an opportunity to benefit from the misfortune — of others, especially in a Civil War of Lies. In fact, isn't that the whole point of a war?

At least the Tricky Traders think so.

The Boy is forced to pass up their offer to join the Passing Pickpockets (he can't afford the membership fee), a decision he is to immediately regret.

The Kettle is boiling. Overcrowded and hot during the day, it turns into a house of bad dreams at night, with the constant hum of gnashing and mourning and the collective nightmare of the inmates rising to the tin roof.

Wild rumours make their rounds; everyone is suspicious of each other. Aunty continues to rant in rhyme with no reason, her band of important Peons regularly threatens them, and they are constantly hungry. Their waking hours are spent scheming; how to get more food and how to get out of the Kettle Camp, all to no purpose. Enemies are made and grudges are kept; threats exchanged and blows traded.

Except during a game of Silly Cricket. Here temporary peace holds

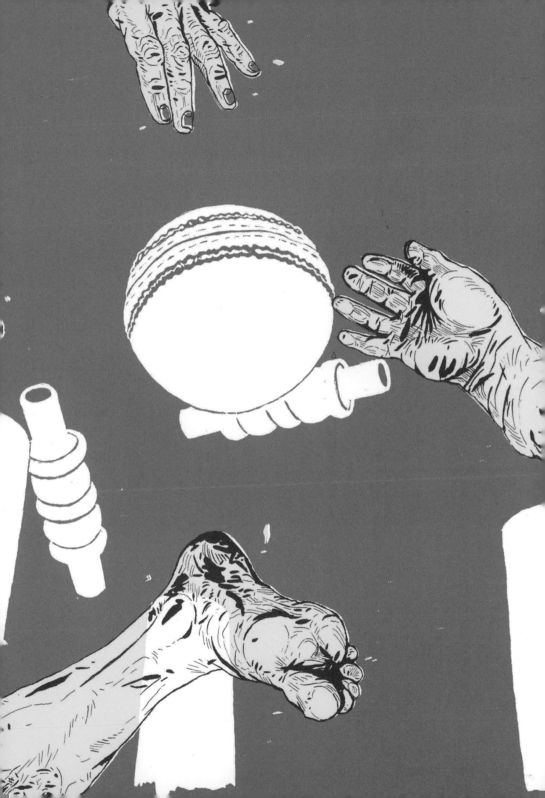

and silliness prevails as the inmates defend some old packing with a worm-eaten plank against any available round object thrown at high speed. Clearly, a silly way for anyone to spend their time.

But the Boy discovers a game of Silly Cricket can be fun, especially when the numbers get relentless. Besides, he sees it as the best way to keep out of the way of Aunty. Her pimples have subsided but the memory of their last meeting stays with him for a long time.

Soon he is belting 4s, 6s and 8s to the far corners of the camp. He also has a peculiar bowling action; a delivery that explodes under the batsmen, and comes to be known as the 'Johny Mine'.

The Boy is thankful he doesn't have to take part in the Reducing Roll-Call (since it doesn't include numbers) called at odd hours of the day by Aunty. He can only guess at what goes on, but after every Reducing Roll-Call, he finds that the inmates are less somehow. He is at a loss to explain this to the Numbers, who like to sum things up neatly.

It is at the camp that the Boy first hears of the White Van Widows. Every time a white van is spotted, someone vanishes from the camp and another White Van Widow is heard wailing.

An important phone call hastily summons the Lying Lizard, who, of course, lies; he says his Ministry of Internal Revisions has done a thorough investigation and there is no truth to the story of the White Van Widows. But he doesn't rule out the possibility of some women having Bad White Dreams, which, he says, they probably deserve. Anyway, there is nothing his Ministry can do about it besides convene a high-level committee to investigate the matter, he explains smoothly as the inmates hold their noses against his bad breath.

The Lizard asks them to forget these Bad White Dreams; he has something far more important to announce: the annual seven-a-side big match (as smiley faces rise from his tail) between the inmates and the Peons.

Aunty makes it clear it is an important match. The press would be in attendance. Everyone is to be on his/her best behaviour. No questions are to be asked.

The Peons have their own announcements to make. They have never lost a match ever, says one Peon imperiously, looking challengingly at the inmates. "Only because it is impossible!" splutters another Peon, going red in the face. At which the lot of them — even Impractical and Impotent — in one voice chorus "Impossible!"

The inmates know their chances of winning *are* impossible, even with the Boy on their side. Yet, that doesn't stop them from practising as often as they can.

There are additional challenges to playing Silly Cricket peculiar to the Kettle Camp. For one, they have to worry about losing limbs as much as losing wickets; the Kettle is surrounded by land mines. For another, the inmates (and some star Silly Cricketers) continue to vanish — some in the daytime. Despite all that the Lizard has said, the Bad White Dreams don't stop.

10

It is the Boy's seventh match, when he hears a loud cheer, as he hits the ball far and away. It is Aunty and her usual frown has been replaced by a silly smile.

It turns out to be a match in which he scores an 8 in the final ball of the final over, and this is when Aunty first strikes up a conversation with the Boy Who Speaks in Numbers. (Well, not quite a conversation since one spoke in colour and the other only in numbers and the memory of their first encounter hasn't been completely forgotten; it is more an exchange of batting averages, which soon extends to a stiff discussion on the odds of the Island of Short Memories, getting into the next Silly World Cup.)

Enough to convince the Boy that Aunty is indeed a Cricket Silly, i.e a person to whom the number of wickets taken matters more than any lives lost.

Then one day Aunty receives an important phone call. Her son calls to say he has decided to leave the Army of the Winning Team. He is catching the bus home to Aunty. Killing hasn't come easily to him. He couldn't bring himself to pull the trigger, especially when he could see his own fear mirrored in the eyes of the enemy: the Little Tin Soldiers. He concludes that the numbers never add up in a war. It doesn't matter which side is counting.

It is the first time anyone in the camp had heard of her son. He is stationed somewhere near the FDL, the Peons are informed by the highly excited Aunty.

There was a time when her son had dreams of playing in the Silly World Cup. No sooner had he left school than he was forced to exchange his bat for a gun and join the Army of the Winning Team. (Just like her husband, who had been one of the first in their village to sign up, and one of the first to die, the Peons explain importantly.)

Aunty lovingly makes her son's favourite sweets and her way to the bus-stop, wearing a silly smile. A silly tune plays in her head. Aunty takes little bites from the sweets while she waits. She stays there till all the sweets are over. It begins to rain but she doesn't mind. She is there all night.

The next morning the Peons meet her with the news that a bus carrying soldiers returning from the frontline has been blown up. When she is brought back to the Kettle she is sneezing and rambling in rhyme with no reason:

Rain rain
Go Little Johnny
Wants to play!
The wheels of the bus
Go round and
A-tishoo a-tishoo!
We all fall down!

From that day Aunty doesn't care about getting pimples. She steadily loses interest in running the Kettle Camp and increasingly the Peons take over. For all her importance she is no different from the other mothers missing a child. Like them Aunty spends all her time hoping. She is hoping for a bus that never comes.

11

If you have survived this story so far, you won't be surprised to hear that the inmates of the Kettle are barely hanging on. You will know well that feeling of listlessness and wanting to hear the end of it.

But then you know that there is no use blaming anyone but yourself, for concerning yourself with the matters of the Boy Who Speaks in Numbers and his unfortunate fellow refugees. You, of all people, having lived as you have in this Island of Short Memories for so long, should know to mind your own business.

The camp is running out of food and water. Uneasy alliances form, as the inmates start sharing their tragedies and exchanging tales of misfortune. The son of the Cook who cries in Silence starts romancing the daughter of the Barber with a Bad Mood, and violence breaks out: no one can stand to see two people finding love amidst all this sadness.

Then one day, the Little Tin Soldiers pay the camp a visit.

They have been seen around the Kettle, but have kept their distance till now. They march onto the field, right in the middle of an important Silly Cricket match. They had already taken one child from each family but have come to the Kettle Camp looking for more recruits. They say they will take anyone, however little.

They try their best to look fierce but are too young to be convincing. They are dressed rather funnily; one pant leg hitched up, an outsize gun on their shoulders, ammunition draped like a necklace. They don't fit the mould of typical soldiers, thinks the Boy.

They don't waste time in their recruitment drive; one keeps guard as the other picks out five young boys and girls. The third, who looks like the leader, calls out to the Boy. But the Boy keeps his head down, trying to ignore him. He looks about the same age as him.

He feels a hard shove from a gun barrel. "Hey! You deaf?" he is asked. There is a sharp intake from off field, followed by:

> *Pat a cake, pat a cake*
> *As fast as you can,*
> *Georgie Porgie pudding and pie*
> *Cut off their tails and made them cry!*

The Little Tin Soldiers look fearfully at where the menacing yet meaningless rhyme comes from.

Aunty is marching onto the field, while the Peons — from Impish to Imperious — try to discourage her. Her perfectly round cheeks are quivering. The Little Tin Soldiers and the Boy Who Speaks in Numbers try not to stare at her pimples.

There are a few tense moments with threats exchanged, then a deal proposed and prices agreed on. The Little Tin Soldiers get to keep the others but not the Boy. Much as they grumble, there is no arguing with Important Aunty.

They give her a mechanical salute as they leave with their tearful new recruits. The Boy is glad Aunty is back in charge at the Kettle Camp but he has a funny feeling that the Little Tin Soldiers too will be back someday.

12

The Boy Who Speaks in Numbers never knew how Mad Uncle and his Mynah came to the Kettle. Someone says he has been a Tricky Trader who lost everything and deserved to do so. Others say he was a poor farmer who saw his family and paddy fields go up in flames. All they know for certain is that the Mynah sings:

Pyre, pyre!
I am on fire!
My village got caught
In a cross-fire!

At which Mad Uncle gets very agitated.

The Aunty calls an important meeting and decides to send Mad Uncle and his Mynah away, but no one will have them. The Mynah keeps singing. Till one day word comes that she will soon be sent to solitary bird confinement.

Life at the Kettle assumes a melancholy monotony. Tempers and food run short. The son of the Cook who cries in Silence runs off with the daughter of Barber with a Bad Mood, right into the arms of the Little Tin Soldiers. This is the only time the Boy has seen the Barber cry.

The Peons know Aunty has to do something to ease the tension. They persuade her to arrange a Rap-for-the-Refugees party just after the big match. There is much excitement in the camp over the announcement that Aunty is throwing a Rap-for-the-Refugees party.

The day of the big match comes. Despite a big score by the Boy, the inmates are finally bowled out by the Peons in a match full of questionable decisions and bad breath. After all, it is the Lizard who is the umpire, although he has never umpired a match before. (He wasn't going to miss an opportunity to impress the ladies or recruit Zero Heroes.)

No one argues with the results. They wisely decide instead to enjoy the Rap-for-the-Refugees party.

The inmates have taken a lot of trouble over their appearance. They wear their best clothes; in most cases, all they have, and as a result, look both larger and older as they stiffly make their way into the tin hall. Mad Uncle is dressed all in black with a dash of yellow to match his Mynah. Aunty sports one polka dot dress over another, over half a track pant, all topped off with a big bow.

The Peons, not to be left behind — even Importunate and Impatient — wear sashes and turbans to signal their position. The Boy Who Speaks in Numbers, on the other hand, has only his favourite Silly World Cup T-shirt.

At one end of the hall is a banner praising the Aunty, with a picture of her; her perfectly round cheeks glowing from the vinyl. At the other end, DJ Pop Pop, the famous DJ/Rapper, has set up station, amidst a tangle of coloured lights and big speakers that dwarf him.

Violently coloured drinks circulate (the more colorful the more deadly), along with a few measly pieces of something fried that disappear fast. No one seems to object to the music being too loud. The press has only kind things to say about Aunty.

Knock, knock!
It's DJ Pop Pop!
In my books
Your top top...

It starts off stiffly, but soon DJ Pop Pop has everyone popping, with the dance floor growing steadily larger till it fills the tin hall, leaving only a few shy inmates still pasted against the tin walls. The dance

steps grow more and more agitated as the Peons — including Imperious and Impractical — join the fray. Turbans and sashes are thrown in the air and even a track pant.

The Lizard tries to grab the microphone, but DJ Pop Pop will have none of it:

> *... but honey you're*
> *asking for*
> *a slap slap!*

he sings, wrestling the microphone back from the Lizard.

Then the Mynah — still in solitary bird confinement — starts shouting 'fire, fire!' but they all ignore it, till they feel the heat seek them out and the fire surround them. Very soon the Rap-for-Refugees party turns into a riot. The Kettle is in flames.

There is a wild stampede as the big speakers come crashing down and the lights go bouncing all over the hall. DJ Pop Pop flees saying "things are too hot hot!" for him. The banner in praise of Aunty is on fire and swinging dangerously over the heads of the panicking inmates.

The last thing the Boy sees as he dives for the floor is the picture of Aunty with her hair in flames, sailing right at him. He thinks he hears:

> *Polly put the kettle on*
> *London Bridge*
> *is falling down,*
> *Polly put the kettle on*
> *Humpty Dumpty*
> *It's time for tea!*

But Aunty is nowhere to be seen.

13

The Kettle is hissing and spitting, soot and smoke covering the tin sheds. Electricity has been cut off. There is talk that food rations have been stopped. The cricket grounds look lonely and sadder than ever, with press passes scattered around. The press has a field day. 'Rude rap for refugees!' scream the headlines.

Stray dogs roam in packs. Everything smells burnt. The TV crews have gone. Posters have come up in the camp. They simply say: 'Leave!'

The Little Tin Soldiers have moved into the camp, making use of the confusion. They too have posters. 'Last Chance for Liberation' says one as they prepare for yet another recruitment drive.

Aunty is in custody. The important files are gone. No important phone calls come. The Important Peons — even Imperious and Impotent — have fled. Even the Numbers look suspicious. That's quite unlike Numbers, thinks the Boy to himself. Numbers by nature are very trusting, he knows.

The Boy sees something flutter to the ground from the Question Tree. It is an old question, now faded and barely readable:

'Is War a Wholesale Business?'

The Boy realises his days here are numbered. He knows that if he stays here at the Kettle Camp, he will never get any answers; he will stay an Ignorant Disillusioned Person (IDP).

14

The Little Tin Soldiers are set on taking the Boy with them this time. But before they can, the Travelling Refugees Circus comes to their camp.

The Circus started with just one act — the Mean Mahout and his Three-legged Elephant — which proved instantly popular. After the elephant died, so did the circus. Only to be revived after the Tricky Traders realised its potential and more talented refugees became available. Now the Circus is famous for the legendary One-Eyed Sharp Shooters, Sorry the Clown, the Jaipur Foot Jugglers, the Terrible Trapeze Act and the Landmine Lady who blows herself up every night. Then there is the Well of Death, in which the rider has to dodge grenades and small arms fire.

The Landmine Lady, since taking over as ringmaster, has brought a sense of theatre that had been previously lacking. It is she who came up with the new name for the circus — The Travelling Refugees Circus. Her act, whilst painful to watch and messy to clean up, has become the highlight of the show.

The Boy Who Speaks in Numbers and some others from the Kettle, including the Barber with a Bad Mood, quickly enlist in the Circus. The Barber is part of a new act, the Close Shave, which involves razor blades. The Boy becomes famous as the Numbr Tumblr.

The Boy discovers it's true what they say about small numbers being different to big numbers; small numbers find happiness in little things, like the Travelling Refugee Circus. So does the Boy.

The overnight sensation, however, is the Constantly Complaining Cow.

Bored at not having anyone to complain to, she is easily persuaded by talent scouts who came to the Small Village of Fat Hopes to audition for the show Refugee Idol. Though she does not win the hotly contested finals, she is signed on by Fugee Records and her complaints climb the charts. Having overcome her reluctance to travel, she soon finds herself with the Travelling Refugees Circus, pleased both to be reunited with the Boy and at the chance to promote her debut album.

The Constantly Complaining Cow takes to the ring after everybody else has finished their acts: after the One-eyed Sharp Shooters has shot a papaw off a child's head, the Barber with a Bad Mood has thrown a tantrum, after Sorry the Clown has apologised for his bad jokes, the Jaipur Foot Jugglers have juggled grenades and mangoes, after the Well of Death proves true to its name, and the Terrible Trapeze Act gets booed off, and finally, after the Numbr Tumblr tames the numbers and the Landmine Lady blows herself up.

The Cow starts innocently enough, reminding them of the price of a packet of milk, at which the audience shake their head in disbelief. The price of diesel has them grumbling, they groan their disapproval at the price of sugar, and boo loudly when she speaks of the price of rice. Soon, they are on their feet cheering and howling. She gets louder with each new revelation, with the audience hanging on to her every grunt and snort.

Just when the audience thinks things can't get worse, she pulls out another example of how it has.

"Are they being told that happiness comes at a price? Or is it simply beyond them?" No one is really sure. All they know is that someone cares.

Large posters announce her arrival ahead. 'The Constantly Complaining Cow! Watch her take the Cost of Lying by the horns!'

The Tricky Traders try getting tips from her, the politicians want to get friendly with her, National Cowgraphic does a feature on her; there is even talk of starting a political party. Every time the Cost of Lying (COL) goes up, so does the popularity of the Constantly Complaining Cow.

The relocated girls from the Gossip Well are among the Cow's biggest fans and mob her after each show.

15

Then one day the Civil War of Lies comes to an abrupt end. The bullets run out before the lies do.

But soon everyone realises that a war doesn't end when you win a battle. It is an awkward moment in the history of the Island. The government has no choice but to set up a commission chaired by the Lying Lizard and comprising a fading cockatoo, a smooth-talking orangutan and a notorious wild boar. It comes to be known as the Z.O.O. (Zero Objectivity, Obviously) Commission.

The Z.O.O. Commission gets off to a shaky start. The Boy Who Speaks in Numbers who insists on appearing before it, suggests that the best way to resolve the mistrust between the warring parties is for them to meet on a cricket pitch. That way it would be easy to see that they are all on the same side — that they are all losers in a war, he tries explaining. His suggestion is met with screeches and snorts of derision.

The Boy's other suggestion that everyone in the Island be taught to speak in numbers is difficult for even the Lizard to ignore. It is an opportunity for the Government to show they are keen to understand Numbers — and sincere about reconciling the differing accounts of the war.

Yet, it is clear the Numbers are not in their favour and no one is surprised when the Z.O.O. Commission is disbanded.

Shortly thereafter, the Government decides to elect a new Prime Minister. Now it would be nice to tell you that the Travelling Refugees Circus registered as a political party, with the Boy Who Speaks in Numbers as candidate for Prime Minister. But the truth is the election is rigged and the candidate sponsored by the Checkpoint Corporation wins by a landslide.

The new Prime Minister repeats 'let bygones be bygones'. True enough, for, there are a lot of new roads and highways, but the checkpoints haven't gone away. They instead have got bigger and more efficient. They have extended their facilities to include a drive through and overnight stay. Checkpoint Hotels are frantically built, able to accommodate large numbers. It is announced that soon they would have the World's Tallest Checkpoint, which would be the first thing travellers see when they come to the Island of Short Memories.

Of the many images and cutouts of the Prime Minister that come to cover the Island of Short Memories, the most popular is of him manning a checkpoint AK47 at the ready, stopping traffic. By such milestones and landmarks, the Prime Minister hopes to convince the people that a new era of peace has been ushered in.

Zero Heroes Day is celebrated lavishly. There is even a Reducing Roll-Call to mark the day. Only Mad Uncle and his Mynah — reunited after the Mynah was temporarily in protective bird custody — question the expenses involved.

The White Van Widows can be heard wailing still. However much the Ministry of Internal Revisions insists it all was a bad dream, their numbers only grow and grow and grow.

16

The Boy Who Speaks in Numbers is on his way to yet another sold-out show of the Travelling Refugees Circus, arranged as part of Zero Heroes Day celebration. Yet, every time he passes a checkpoint, he gets an uneasy feeling of still not belonging. They bring back memories of the Singing Fridges Checkpoint and a shudder along with it.

The Travelling Refugees Circus gets a rousing reception at its destination. It is exactly like the camps they have played at before, except it isn't called a camp. It is called a Resettled Village. The inmates, however, look more unsettled than resettled.

The Boy changes for the show, but despite a false mustache he still doesn't cut a heroic figure, not with his finger up his nose. He is thinking of how lonely he has become, but no tears come. He is reminded again of the riddle his uncle had asked him — "What is it that counts for something, yet really stands for nothing?" It comes to him the answer is 'Zero', yet the realisation is not accompanied by a sense of triumph, but with a sense of acute loss.

Ever since a local milk company sponsored the Constantly Complaining Cow, she has had less time for the Travelling Refugees Circus and no time to worry about the Cost of Lying. After the release of her second album, she is increasingly seen in the company of Tricky Traders and politicians. It isn't long before she is announced as Minister in charge of the newly formed Ministry of Complaining Affairs. (The Honorable Constantly Complaining Cow is unavailable to comment on this story, her privately complaining secretary says.)

Then comes news of Important Aunty. After an enquiry, all charges against her are dropped, but now that the camps are officially closed, Aunty has no job. Shortly after that, she is arrested for loitering at a bus stop. Her lawyers explain the important role she once played and she is released with a warning by the judge. Aunty promptly heads back to the bus stop. She doesn't see the speeding bus till it is too late.

For his contribution to the sorry state of affairs, the Lizard is rewarded with a job in an advertising agency run by a Minister's daughter-in-law. He goes on to create the campaign 'Drive South, Drive Safe' but is arrested for drunk driving on his way to the presentation. It results in a slight delay in the launch, but the campaign is a great success. Though there is no noticeable decline in the number of road accidents, it wins the agency a number of awards.

17

The big tent soon starts filling up, and the audience of Ignorant Deceived People (IDPs) dutifully take their seats. It is evident they have given up on believing and have surrendered to their fate; not clear whom to trust, not sure whom to blame, only knowing that they are a long way from home.

The Landmine Lady introduces the first act, the One-eyed Sharp Shooters, who shoot a papaw perched on a child's head in half and then promptly eat it without offering any to the child.

The Sharp Shooters are followed by the Barber who is in such a bad mood, he nearly slits the throat of a member of the audience.

Next on is Sorry the Clown who apologises in advance for his poor jokes.

By the time the Terrible Trapeze comes on, the air is thick with gunpowder and children grumbling, with the crowd wanting more action.

Soon, there is a loud boo signalling the Trapeze Act has come to a hurried end. Shortly, the leader of the trapeze troupe is carried out moaning loudly, holding his head at an odd angle. He has missed the safety net again. The crowd cheers his exit.

The Landmine Lady announces the Numbr Tumblr. The crowd cheers even louder. It is time for the Boy Who Speaks in Numbers to enter the ring. It is time to take his finger out of his nose.

The Boy is halfway through his act when the rains come down. But this is no monsoon rain. It doesn't just thunder, it shrieks and howls and weeps.

Those caught outside the Big Tent say it tastes of tears. The White Van Widows swear they hear the cries of their loved ones.

The rains prowls and swirls and tears through the holes in the tent, threatening to bring the tent down, leaving everyone cowering in fear. The One-eyed Sharp Shooters fire wildly into the air. Sorry the Clown is sobbing uncontrollably. The Terrible Trapeze looks terrified. It is the first time the Boy has seen the Barber so scared. Even the children fall silent and cling to their parents. The Boy loses his false mustache, but no one notices.

Yet he is not afraid; he knows he can count on the numbers.

The same numbers that witnessed checkpoints come and villages go up in flames, cows who complain and lizards with bad breath.

The very numbers that met with Important Peons and an Aunty who scolded in rhyme with no reason.

The numbers that watched the Boy escape landmines and the Little Tin Soldiers — only to get bowled out in cricket.

The numbers that were by the side of the Boy at the Travelling Refugees Circus.

He knows the numbers will have the last word.

The rain keeps wailing and mourning and clamouring to be let into the big tent, refusing to let up for six nights. Finally, on the seventh day it ceases and they make their way out in the uneasy silence that follows.

Everything has been brought to the ground including the check points — even the world's tallest checkpoint. They no longer look threatening. Soggy cutouts of the Prime Minister — AK47 at the ready — lie under feet as the people make their way back to their Resettled Villages.

Not all has been destroyed by the rain; at every town square and in every village junction throughout the Small Island of Short Memories, they discover an ugly tree flowering. It has a bittersweet and long-forgotten scent. It is flowering with questions.

ACKNOWLEDGEMENTS

My thanks to Carm3n and Richard
for initially publishing this as a short story.

Tracy and M1nd Adventures Th3atre Company for turning it into a play,
Ruwanthi3, Tracy again, Steve and the whole cast of Travelling Circus
for taking this further than my wildest imagining —
all the way to the Hindu Metroplus Theatr3 Fest in Chenna1.

Sandra for typing a mill1ooooooon drafts.

Jeeevani, Roel and Saroja
for being w1lling readers and able ed1tors.

Ranjan and R1chard for keeping th3 faith.

Ala1n and N1a for introducing me to Tara Books.

Ge3tha for turning a traumatised Boy into an assured storytell3r.
Gita, Rathna and Matthew for shaping this into an exquisite read.

To my Lord for answering my prayers —
over and abov3 my expectations!

REVIEWS

"A star is born! The Constantly Complaining Cow breaks the stereotype of boring bovines!"

Moo Mason, Editor, *National Cowgraphic*

"We condemn the portrayal of our client, especially the allegations of bad breath in this book. Our client brushes his teeth a dozen times a day. Sometimes more."

Longden and Libel, Lawyers for the Lying Lizard

"Having done a thorough check of our membership rolls, we can confirm that no Lying Lizard is enlisted in our member agencies. Our membership conform to the highest ethical standards and practise an honorable profession."

President, Advertising Association

"An important record of the political rise and grassroots support enjoyed by the Travelling Refugees Circus. We recommend every member buys a copy of the book."

Spokesperson for the Travelling Refugees Circus